FREDDIE

Based on *The Railway Series* **by the Rev. W. Awdry**

Illustrations by
Robin Davies and Jerry Smith

EGMONT

EGMONT

We bring stories to life

First published in Great Britain in 2006
by Egmont UK Limited
239 Kensington High Street, London W8 6SA
This edition published in 2008
All Rights Reserved

Thomas the Tank Engine & Friends™

CREATED BY BRITT ALLCROFT

Based on the Railway Series by the Reverend W Awdry
© 2008 Gullane (Thomas) LLC. A HIT Entertainment company.
Thomas the Tank Engine & Friends and Thomas & Friends are trademarks of Gullane (Thomas) Limited.
Thomas the Tank Engine & Friends and Design is Reg. U.S. Pat. & Tm. Off.

HiT entertainment

ISBN 978 1 4052 3492 4
1 3 5 7 9 10 8 6 4 2
Printed in Italy

The Forest Stewardship Council (FSC) is an international, non-governmental organisation
dedicated to promoting responsible management of the world's forests. FSC operates a
system of forest certification and product labelling that allows consumers to identify
wood and wood-based products from well managed forests.

For more information about Egmont's paper buying policy please visit www.egmont.co.uk/ethicalpublishing

For more information about the FSC please visit their website at www.fsc.uk.org

*T*his is a story about Fearless Freddie. Everyone had heard tales of Fearless Freddie. He thought he was the fastest engine in all of Sodor. But then Rheneas and Skarloey challenged Freddie to a race …

One day, an old friend was returning to the Narrow Gauge Railway. His name was Fearless Freddie. He was fast, fun and . . . fearless!

Thomas brought Freddie to the Transfer Yards.

"Hello, Sir Handel," wheeshed Freddie.

"Hello, Freddie!" whistled Sir Handel. "I haven't seen you for years."

"Fearless Freddie is back!" puffed Freddie.

"I didn't know you two were friends," peeped Thomas.

"Oh yes," puffed Sir Handel. "Freddie was the fastest engine in the hills!"

Suddenly, Rheneas and Skarloey raced into the Yards.

"I'm the winner!" peeped Skarloey.

"No, I am!" wheeshed Rheneas.

"Who are you?" pouted Freddie.

"We're the fastest engines in the hills!" chimed Skarloey.

"I'll show you who's fastest," boasted Freddie. "I'll race you down the mountain." Freddie was sure he was going to win.

Freddie huffed and puffed up the mountain. It was harder than he remembered.

"Flatten my funnel!" he wheeshed. "I used to be able to chuff up here in no time."

Rheneas and Skarloey were waiting to start the race. Freddie puffed in slowly.

"All right Fearless Freddie!" tooted Rheneas. "Ready, steady …"

"Go!" whistled Skarloey.

And they were off.

Freddie was racing very fast, but soon he began to run out of puff.

"Oh, no! Those young engines will bump my buffers!" he chuffed, as he slowed down.

Suddenly, Freddie had an idea. He remembered an old track.

"The Old Rocky Way!" he thought, excitedly. "No one will remember that now."

Freddie steamed down the track. Rheneas and Skarloey did not see that he had taken a short cut.

The tracks on The Old Rocky Way were old and wobbly, but this way was much quicker. Freddie got to the bottom of the mountain in no time.

Rheneas and Skarloey chuffed in.

"You're so fast," wheeshed Rheneas.

"Race you again!" huffed Skarloey. "Please, Fearless Freddie."

"Of course. Fearless Freddie never says no to a race!" boasted Freddie.

Rheneas and Skarloey were soon ready to race again.

"We'll race you down the other side, this time!" said Rheneas.

"The other side of the mountain is very steep," peeped Freddie.

"You're not scared, are you?" teased Skarloey.

"Of course not. I'm Fearless Freddie!" chuffed Freddie. "Off we go!"

Freddie raced ahead of the other engines, but he began to run out of puff again. Fearless Freddie didn't want to lose.

"I can take The Craggy Track and then I will win."

So Freddie took another short cut. The track was old and wobbly just like the last one. Freddie was usually fearless, but this time even he was a little frightened.

Freddie soon arrived at the bottom of the mountain, safe and sound.

But Rheneas and Skarloey were not safe and sound. The track was very steep and Rheneas had raced right off the rails!

Skarloey raced up to Freddie.

"Rheneas has come off the track!" cried Skarloey. "I don't know where he is. We were trying to catch you, Fearless Freddie, but you were too fast."

Freddie knew he hadn't been fast, at all. He had tricked the little engines. And now Rheneas was in trouble.

Sir Handel puffed in with The Thin Controller. He had heard what had happened to Rheneas.

"It's all my fault," sniffed Freddie. Freddie told everyone how he had won the races.

"You tricked us!" tooted Skarloey. "And now Rheneas is lost and in trouble."

"No, he isn't!" whistled Freddie, loudly. "I can find him. I know all the tracks. Please Sir, follow me."

And so Freddie steamed away to rescue Rheneas.

Freddie knew another forgotten track, The Old Mountainside Run. He led the rescue party down to the valley. And there was Rheneas!

"I'm so happy you've found me," peeped Rheneas.

"So am I," puffed Freddie.

The Thin Controller, the Fireman, Freddie, Sir Handel and Skarloey pulled Rheneas back on to the track.

All the engines chuffed cheerfully back to the Transfer Yards.

"I'm sorry I tricked you," puffed Freddie. "You're much faster engines than me."

"But you know all the old tracks," peeped Rheneas. "Please tell us about them."

So Freddie began to tell the young engines tales about the old tracks.

Everyone was happy that Fearless Freddie was back.

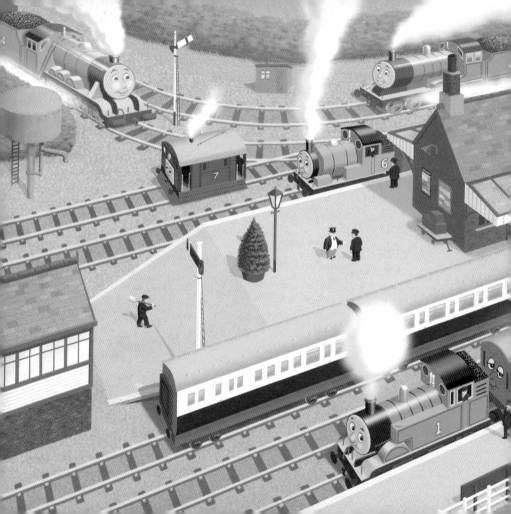

The Thomas Story Library is THE definitive collection of stories about Thomas and ALL his friends.

5 more Thomas Story Library titles will be chuffing into your local bookshop in August 2008!

Jeremy
Hector
BoCo
Billy
Whiff

And there are even more Thomas Story Library books to follow late
So go on, start your Thomas Story Library NOW!

A Fantastic Offer for Thomas the Tank Engine Fans!

Thomas

STICK
POUND
COIN
HERE

In every Thomas Story Library book like this one, you will find a special token. Collect 6 Thomas tokens and we will send you a brilliant Thomas poster, and a double-sided bedroom door hanger! Simply tape a £1 coin in the space above, and fill out the form overleaf.

TO BE COMPLETED BY AN ADULT

To apply for this great offer, ask an adult to complete the coupon below and send it with a pound coin and 6 tokens, to:
THOMAS OFFERS, PO BOX 715, HORSHAM RH12 5WG

☐ Please send a Thomas poster and door hanger. I enclose 6 tokens plus a £1 coin. (Price includes P&P)

Fan's name...

Address...

....Postcode............................

Date of birth..

Name of parent/guardian...

Signature of parent/guardian...

Please allow 28 days for delivery. Offer is only available while stocks last. We reserve the right to change the terms of this offer at any time and we offer a 14 day money back guarantee. This does not affect your statutory rights.

☐ Data Protection Act: If you do not wish to receive other similar offers from us or companies we recommend, please tick this box. Offers apply to UK only.